The Mouse and the Moon

The Mouse and the Moon

Gabriel Alborozo

Henry Holt and Company
NEW YORK

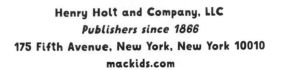

Henry Holt and Company, LLC
Publishers since 1866
175 Fifth Avenue, New York, New York 10010
mackids.com

Henry Holt® is a registered trademark of Henry Holt and Company, LLC.
Copyright © 2016 by Gabriel Alborozo
All rights reserved.

Library of Congress Cataloging-in-Publication Data
Names: Alborozo, 1972- author, illustrator.
Title: The mouse and the moon / Gabriel Alborozo.
Description: First edition. | New York : Henry Holt and Company, 2016. |
Summary: "A mouse wants to meet the moon, but finds a
surprising new friend instead"–Provided by publisher.
Identifiers: LCCN 2015030951 | ISBN 9781627792240 (hardback)
Subjects: | CYAC: Mice–Fiction. | Moon–Fiction. | Friendship–Fiction. |
BISAC: JUVENILE FICTION / Social Issues / Friendship. | JUVENILE FICTION /
Animals / Mice, Hamsters, Guinea Pigs, etc. | JUVENILE FICTION / Social
Issues / Emotions & Feelings.
Classification: LCC PZ7.1.A43 Mo 2016 | DDC [E]–dc23
LC record available at http://lccn.loc.gov/2015030951

Our books may be purchased in bulk for promotional, educational, or business use.
Please contact your local bookseller or the Macmillan Corporate and
Premium Sales Department at (800) 221-7945 ext. 5442 or by e-mail
at MacmillanSpecialMarkets@macmillan.com.

First Edition—2016 / Designed by April Ward
The illustrations for this book were created with
pen and ink and watercolor, enhanced digitally.

Printed in China by RR Donnelley Asia Printing Solutions Ltd.,
Dongguan City, Guangdong Province

1 3 5 7 9 10 8 6 4 2

For my family

In a dark and broken tree,
in a dark and wild wood,
there lived a little mouse.
All alone.

His only friend was
the moon.

Each night the moon appeared,
the little mouse would talk to his
friend about his news, his hopes,
and his fears.

But the moon never replied.

The little mouse wondered if maybe the moon was just too far away to hear him.

So the little mouse set off to find his friend.

The little mouse
ran and ran through
the wild wood.

The moon was always above, and it didn't get any closer.

Soon the mouse was as far from home as he'd ever been. He was feeling a little afraid.

The little mouse stopped
to rest.
   He searched the night sky
for his friend, but the moon
was nowhere to be seen.
Until . . .

"Hello?" a small voice whispered, so quietly that, even with his big ears, the little mouse could barely hear it.

The mouse crept forward and peered around a tree.

"Hello?" the little
mouse called back.

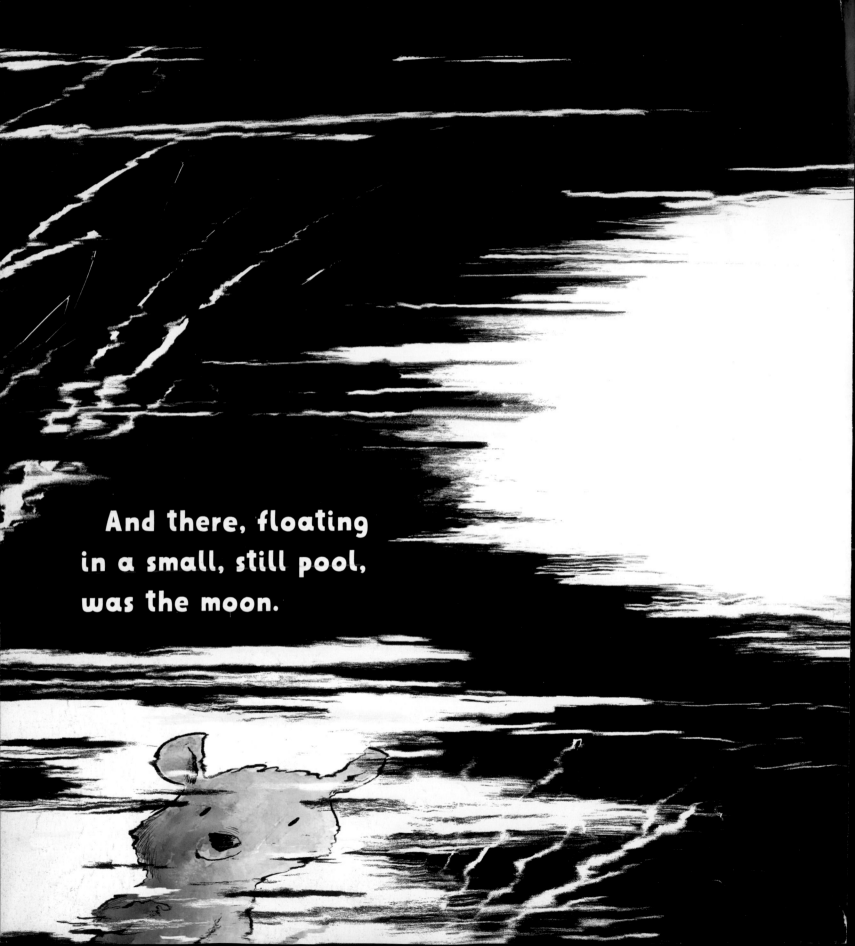

And there, floating
in a small, still pool,
was the moon.

The mouse couldn't believe it! He'd found his friend at last!

Hidden from sight, beneath the moon's reflection, there lived a tiny fish.

The tiny fish couldn't believe it! His friend the moon was speaking to him at last!

"Me too!" squeaked the little mouse. "I'm so glad to meet you!"

They stayed up all
night talking of this and
that, and that and this.

As they talked, the sky
became lighter and lighter.
Dawn was coming.
The sky brightened, and
the moon grew fainter.

"Oh no!" they both cried.
"Please don't go!"

The little mouse
moved as close as he
could to the moon.

The tiny fish swam up
as close as he dared.

Then the moon vanished,

and the two new friends saw
each other for the first time.

One above.

One below.

Both together.
And both happy.